SECRETS OF THE LIBRARY OF DOOM

THE
ERASER STRIKES BACK

BY MICHAEL DAHL

ILLUSTRATED BY PATRICIO CLAREY

STONE ARCH BOOKS
a capstone imprint

Secrets of the Library of Doom is published by
Stone Arch Books, an imprint of Capstone.
1710 Roe Crest Drive
North Mankato, Minnesota 56003
www.capstonepub.com

Library of Congress Cataloging-in-Publication Data is
available on the Library of Congress website.

ISBN: 978-1-4965-9722-9 (library binding)
ISBN: 978-1-4965-9901-8 (paperback)
ISBN: 978-1-4965-9741-0 (ebook PDF)

Summary: The Librarian is caught in a deadly trap where a
giant eraser swings above him, getting closer with every swipe.
Can the hero break free before he gets wiped out for good?

Designed by Hilary Wacholz

Printed and bound in the USA.
PA117

TABLE OF CONTENTS

The Library of Doom is a hidden fortress.
It holds the world's largest collection
of strange and dangerous books.

Behold the Librarian. He defends the Library—and
the world—from super-villains, clever thieves,
and fierce monsters. Many of his adventures
have remained secret. Now they can be told.

SECRET #101
SOME STORIES CAN NEVER BE ERASED.

Chapter One

TOWER IN THE STORM

Lightning FLASHES and thunder roars.

A wild storm **BLOWS** through the Mountains of Madness. On one of the mountains stands a dark tower.

The tower looks like a **GIANT** pencil stuck into the rock.

The storm is **LOUD**. But a sound coming from inside the tower is even louder.

AAAAAAAHHAAAAAAHAHAHA!

It is laughter, but it is EVIL.

The one who laughs stands in a huge room at the top of the tower.

"Welcome to my home!" says the ERASER.

The villain has WILD hair and a wide, toothy grin. He looks down into the large room.

A long metal rod hangs from the middle of the ceiling. It swings back and forth with DEADLY force.

SWOOOOOSH! CLICK!

SWOOOOOSH! CLICK!

On the bottom of the rod is a giant red eraser.

The deadly eraser swings above a man strapped to the stone floor. He is the LIBRARIAN.

Chapter Two

EVIL MACHINE

The Eraser stares down at the Librarian.

"You fell for my TRICK," the Eraser says. "No one was in trouble here! I sent you a fake message, calling for help."

The Librarian **PULLS** against the straps on his arms and legs. *Why can't I get free?* he wonders.

"You'll never escape," says the Eraser. "Those straps are made from the spines of ANCIENT books."

The villain points to the walls. "This room is also made from book spines," he says. "You can't **BREAK** through them."

Spines are the hero's one **WEAKNESS**.

He made a promise when he became the Librarian. "I will *never* break a spine," he had said.

The Eraser turns to leave. "Any last words?" he asks. "Anything to say with your final **BREATH**?"

The Librarian is silent.

Above him the giant red eraser swings back and forth. With each swing, the metal rod clicks.

SWOOOOOOSH! CLICK!

SWOOOOOOSH! CLICK!

And with each click, the rod drops a little lower. Soon, the red eraser will be **LOW** enough to touch the Librarian.

Then it will start erasing him out
of the world.

"You've always **RUBBED** me the wrong way," says the Eraser. "Now you'll be rubbed out *forever!*"

He laughs again.

AAAAAAAHHAAAAAAHAHAHA!

Then the villain opens a secret door in one of the spines. He DISAPPEARS.

The Librarian is alone.

The red eraser keeps swinging.

Chapter Three

SWINGING WIDE

The Librarian looks around the room.

The Eraser was right. The wall is made of hundreds of book spines pressed together. And the straps are **TIGHT** around his gloves.

The DEADLY eraser machine swings closer and closer.

The Librarian thinks about what the Eraser said. *Anything to say with your final breath?*

BREATH!

"Maybe that's how I can stop this evil machine," says the hero.

The Librarian **BLOWS** at the giant eraser.

His **POWERFUL** breath hits the eraser.
It makes the eraser swing farther in
each direction.

The eraser swings so far up that it rubs
against the walls. The walls begin to fade
away with every hit.

Soon, there are **OPENINGS** in the room
on each side of the Librarian.

Chapter Four

ANOTHER HERO

Storm winds **BLOW** into the room through the openings.

The Librarian thought the winds would slam into the eraser machine. He thought they would break it. He was wrong.

The DEADLY eraser is still working. It will touch him in two more swings.

"Librarian!" comes a voice.

A woman in red flies through an opening in the wall. It is the SPECIALIST!

The hero soars toward the EVIL machine. She tears the metal rod from the ceiling. Then she throws the eraser to the floor.

The Specialist kneels down and pulls off the Librarian's straps.

"How did you know I was here?" asks the Librarian.

"The VOICES OF DOOM were calling me," says the Specialist. "They call whenever the end of your story is near. I will always be here to help!"

Then the two heroes hear a **SHOUT** near the wall.

"No! No!" SCREAMS the Eraser. He has come through another secret door. "You'll be sorry you came, Specialist."

The Eraser points upward. "Thousands of erasers are hidden in the ceiling," he cries. "With a push of a button, I will destroy—"

GRRRRRRRRRRUUUUNGK

A loud grinding sound suddenly fills the room.

Chapter Five

HANDS ON

Everyone looks at the giant red eraser that the Specialist threw down.

It erased the stones where it fell. It has rubbed a HOLE into the floor.

GRRRRRRRROOOOOMMMMMMM!

With a roar, more of the floor **BREAKS**.

The heroes float into the air. But the Eraser **SLIDES** toward the huge hole.

The Eraser tries to save himself. He grabs a stone sticking out of the wall. But his EVIL eraser machine slides toward him.

The machine **SMASHES** against his hands. They are rubbed out!

AAHHHHHHHEEEEEEEEEE!

The Eraser screams. He falls down into the **DEEP** darkness of the tower.

The two heroes **FLY** down after the villain.

"Watch my new TRICK," the Specialist tells the Librarian. "It's because my circulation has increased."

The Specialist starts to grow larger and larger. She becomes a **GIANT**!

She **FILLS** the inside of the tower and stands several stories tall.

Then the Specialist **REACHES** out. She catches the Eraser with her giant fingers.

"I thought you could use a hand," she says with a smile.

The Specialist and the Librarian **SOAR** out of the tower. The giant hero holds the villain in the palm of her hand.

"Don't worry," the Specialist tells the Eraser. "You'll get your hands back."

"Yes, but only after we *hand* you over to a prison," says the Librarian.

The three rise through the wild storm, heading toward the LIBRARY OF DOOM.

GLOSSARY

circulation (sur-kyoo-LAY-shun)—the movement of the blood through the heart and body (good circulation is a sign of good health); also, how often books are checked out of a library

grinding (GREYEN-ding)—rubbing together in a rough way

machine (mah-SHEEN)—a thing with moving parts that does some type of work

rod (ROD)—a long, thin pole made of wood or metal

spine (SPEYEN)—the part of the book where the pages join together; the spine is the end you see when a book is on a shelf

story (STOHR-ee)—a level of a house or building

strap (STRAHP)—a thin, flat piece of cloth or other material used to hold something down or keep it from moving; also, to hold something with a strap

villain (VIL-uhn)—a person who does bad things and fights against the hero

TALK ABOUT IT

1. Do you like the title of this book? What makes for a good title? Brainstorm other titles that would work for this story.

2. Describe the character of the Specialist. What does she look like? What are her strengths and weaknesses? Use examples to back up your answer.

WRITE ABOUT IT

1. The book starts with the Librarian trapped in a tower. Write a story that explains how the Eraser caught the hero.

2. Look back at the illustrations. Which one do you think works best with the action in the story? Write a paragraph arguing for your choice.

ABOUT THE AUTHOR

Michael Dahl is an award-winning author of more than 200 books for young people. He especially likes to write scary or weird fiction. His latest series are the sci-fi adventure Escape from Planet Alcatraz and School Bus of Horrors. As a child, Michael spent lots of time in libraries. "The creepier, the better," he says. These days, besides writing, he likes traveling and hunting for the one, true door that leads to the Library of Doom.

ABOUT THE ILLUSTRATOR

Patricio Clarey was born in 1978 in Argentina. He graduated in fine arts from the Martín A. Malharro School of Visual Arts, specializing in illustration and graphic design. Patricio currently lives in Barcelona, Spain, where he works as a freelance graphic designer and illustrator. He has created several comics and graphic novels, and his work has been featured in books and other publications.